Trudy
the Tree Frog

JENNIFER KEATS CURTIS

Illustrated by Laura Jacques

Schiffer Publishing Ltd

4880 Lower Valley Road • Atglen, PA 19310

Designed by Danielle D. Farmer
Cover design by Danielle D. Farmer
Type set in Joli Script/BiracDT

ISBN: 978-0-7643-4997-3

Printed in China

Published by Schiffer Publishing, Ltd.
4880 Lower Valley Road
Atglen, PA 19310
Phone: (610) 593-1777; Fax: (610) 593-2002
E-mail: Info@schifferbooks.com

For our complete selection of fine books on this and related
subjects, please visit our website at www.schifferbooks.com.
You may also write for a free catalog.

This book may be purchased from the publisher. Please try
your bookstore first.

We are always looking for people to write books on new and
related subjects. If you have an idea for a book, please contact
us at proposals@schifferbooks.com.

OTHER SCHIFFER BOOKS BY THE AUTHOR

Osprey Adventure, Jennifer Keats Curtis,
ISBN. 978-0-8703-3593-8

Saving Squeak. The Otter Tale, Jennifer Keats Curtis,
ISBN. 978-0-7643-3588-4

Squirrel Rescue, Jennifer Keats Curtis. Illustrated
by Laura Jacques, ISBN. 978-0-7643-4246-2

FOR MY FABULOUS FROG-LOVING FAMILY:
Jim, Maddie, and Max

Jennifer Keats Curtis

MUCH LOVE AND GRATITUDE TO THE CARUSO FAMILY:
Mike, Janet, Michael, Christian, Arianna, Buster,
and especially Abby

Laura Jacques

Trudy the tree frog lived in a tree.
There she slumbered peacefully
Amongst the branches that were her bed,
Until an idea entered her head.

One moonlit night she leapt out wide,
Landed on a window side.
Peered directly through the glass,
With sticky pads, she held on fast.

A child's room,
a glorious sight.
A two-tiered bed,
to her delight.

Fluffy pillows,
sheet tucked tight,
Seemed the thing
for a restful night.

In the top bunk
a young girl read,
Tucked so snugly
in her bed.

Trudy saw her
turn the page,
Knew she needed
to engage.

Trudy croaked loudly, as tree frogs can do.
Got the girl's attention, quickly too.
"Let me in," trilled Trudy wretchedly.
"No more tree, but a bed for me."

The girl heard the call and sat upright,
Came to the window with a flashlight.
Imagine her surprise to see
A green frog clinging restlessly.

"What's the matter, little frog?
You can't come in, you'll wake the dog.
Go back to your tree; it's time to sleep.
Get off my window; take a leap."

"My bed is hard, and thorny too.
But a soft bed like yours would do.
These branches scratch so awfully
And oh, these twigs, they're poking me."

That poor young girl, she scratched her head.
Could she sleep with a frog in her bed?
Would Trudy croak, wake her dad up?
Her mom, her brother, even their pup?

Trudy sprang up the window with a clunk.
"Can't I sleep in the bottom bunk?
I'll be so quiet, not a peep.
Please let me in so I can sleep."

That little girl opened her window wide.

Like a flash, Trudy hopped inside,
Jumped across the floor and into bed.
Made herself comfy, put down her head.

But the bed was too big and poor Trudy too small.
The oversized bunk wasn't frog-sized at all.
Try as she might to snuggle under the sheet,
Bedclothes snagged on her sticky-toed feet.

"This isn't what I thought it'd be,"
Trudy trilled unhappily.
"How can I doze in this awful place?"
She lisped, tongue stuck fast to the pillowcase.

The little girl didn't want Trudy to cry
So she tried singing her a lullaby.
"Rockabye Froggy on the tree top,
Close your eyes, your tears will stop."

But Trudy wailed so piercingly,
That horrid noise woke up Daddy.
He dashed in, turned on the light.
Wasn't everything all right?

He saw a frog in his little girl's room,
Rushed downstairs to get a broom.
Came running back to sweep it out
When she told him what had come about.

They scooped up Trudy carefully.
"Go outside where you should be.
A tree frog's place is in a tree.
Limbs make your bed so perfectly."

They placed Trudy on the sill.
"Thank you," she said, in her trill.
She leapt right back to her tree,
Settled in so cozily.

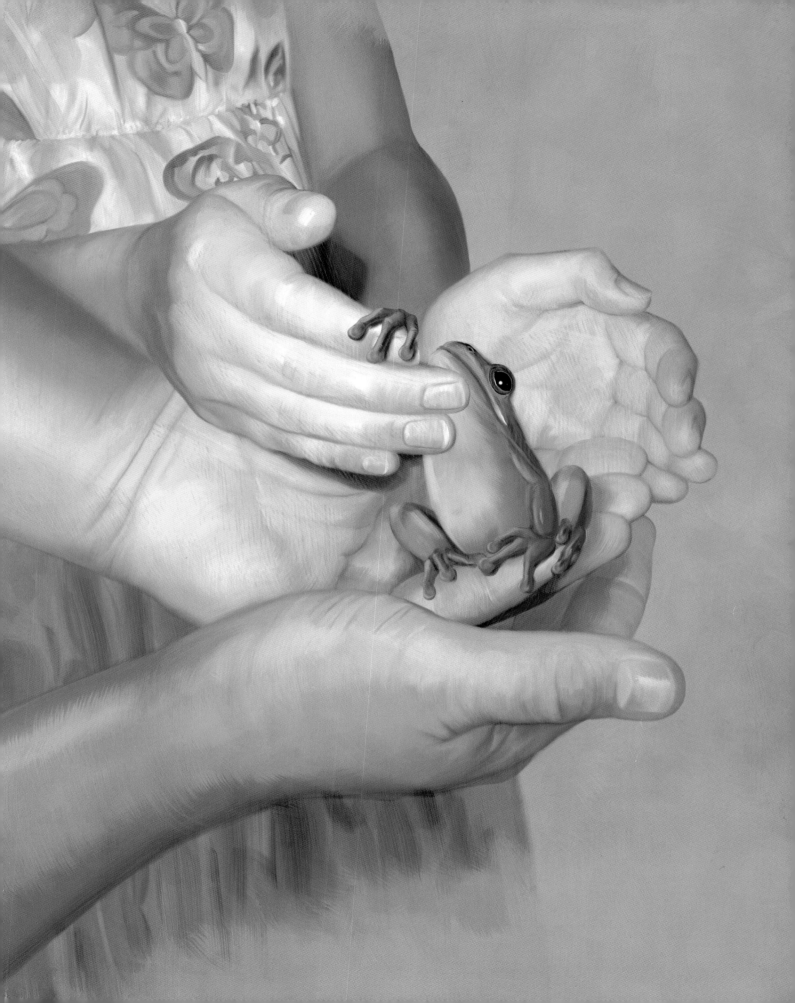

"Good night," croaked Trudy happily,
Contentedly nestled in her tree.
The bark no longer scratched her side.
She liked the leaves that covered her hide.

The girl watched Trudy fall asleep.
Saw her big eyes close, her breathing go deep.
"Good night, little frog," said the girl, and arose,
Then shut her window so Trudy could doze.